Read more from the
SUPER world of

Pizazz

Pizazz Vs The New Kid

Pizazz Vs Perfecto

Pizazz Vs The Demons

Pizazz Vs Everyone

Pizazz Vs The Future

PiZAZZ

VS

THE FUTURE

IT'S NOT EASY
BEING SUPER...

Sophy Henn

SIMON & SCHUSTER

First published in Great Britain in 2023 by Simon & Schuster UK Ltd

Text and illustrations copyright © 2023 Sophy Henn

1 3 5 7 9 10 8 6 4 2

Simon & Schuster UK Ltd
1st Floor, 222 Gray's Inn Road
London WC1X 8HB

www.simonandschuster.co.uk
www.simonandschuster.com.au
www.simonandschuster.co.in

Simon & Schuster Australia, Sydney
Simon & Schuster India, New Delhi

A CIP catalogue record for this book is available from the British Library.

PB ISBN 978-1-3985-0586-5
eBook ISBN 978-1-3985-2863-5
eAudio ISBN 978-1-3985-0588-9

Printed and Bound in the UK using 100% Renewable Electricity
at CPI Group (UK) Ltd

MIX
Paper | Supporting
responsible forestry
FSC® C171272

Grandma AKA RAY
Gramps AKA INFERNO
AUNTY BLAZE
SHE'S SO COOOOOOL
Uncle Teaser
Uncle Titano-ooooo
Jett my super friend
Granny
my secret baddie friend
Aunty FURY
KAPOW

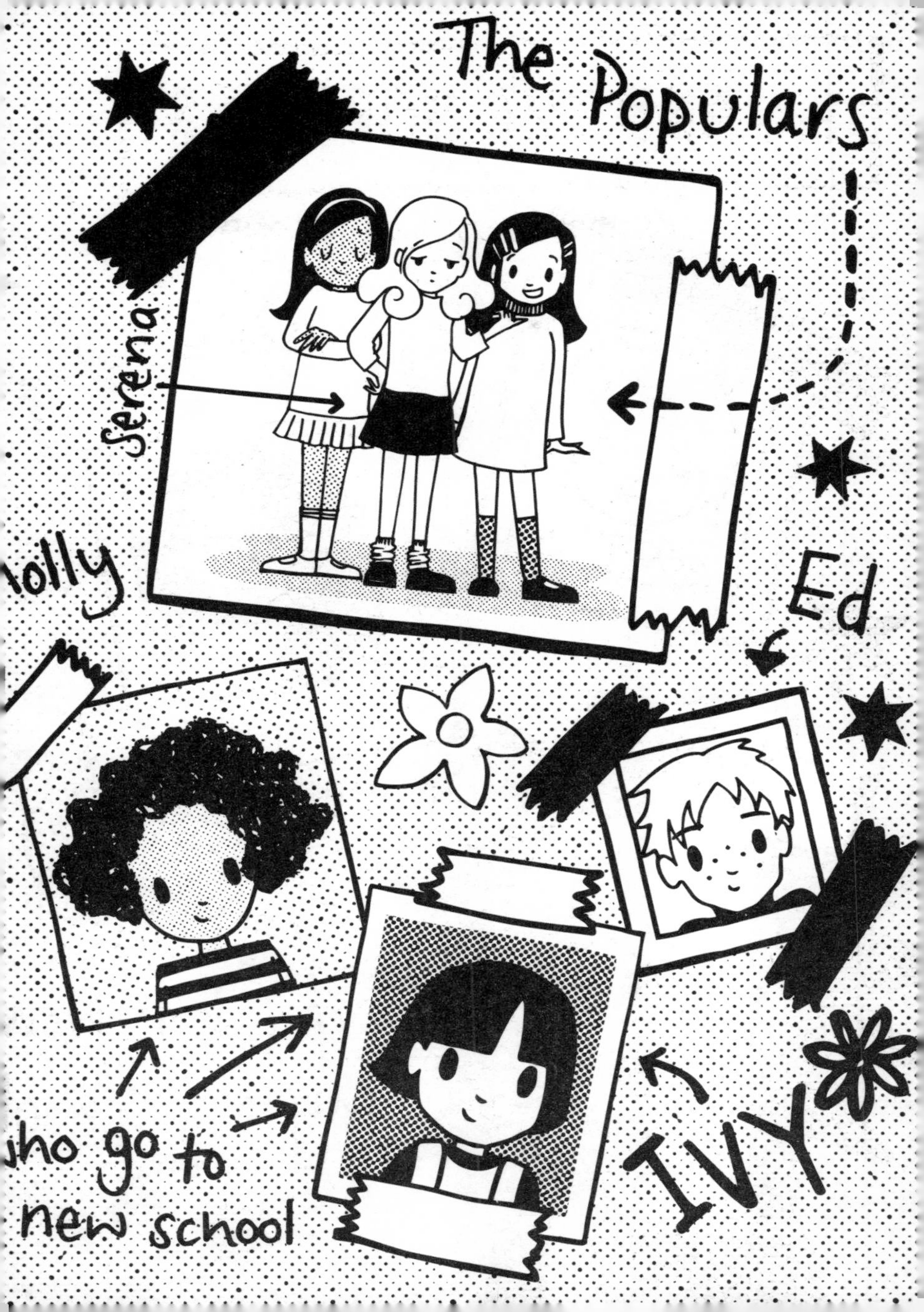
The Populars
Serena
Holly
Ed
IVY
who go to
new school

The bit where I say hello . . .

2

The bit where I . . .

HA HA!

. . . H_A! H_A! Only joking, it's still chapter one and I am still a **SUPERHERO**, only these days it doesn't seem to bother me as much as it used to. I mean, I'm still not *quite* as keen on the idea as the rest of my '**SUPER**' family, but they are *really*, REALLY into it . . . the costumes, the **POWERS**, the defeating **BADDIES**, the saving the world, the eyebrows, the names . . . talking of which, mine is **Pizazz**. AKA PIZAZZ!!! **EYE ROLL**

I know, it's not ideal and I can think of names I would rather be called, like **DYNAMITE**, or **LAZARAMA** or even **GERONIMO**, but when you consider that there is an actual **SUPER** called **FARTERELLA**, then really Pizazz isn't that bad at all. Don't get me **WRONG**, this **SUPER** business can be really . . .

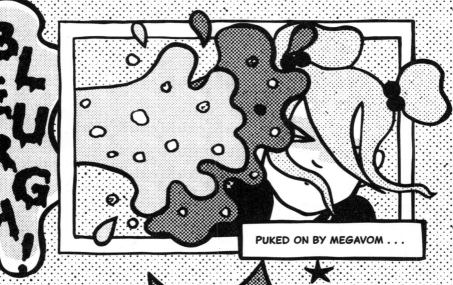

...A BIT
SUPER!!!

FLYING!

... WHICH MEANS YOU CAN ZOOM OFF TO PLUTO IF YOU FANCY SOME PEACE AND QUIET. THERE'S ALMOST NEVER ANYONE ELSE THERE ...

YOU HAVE THIS BUNCH OF **WEIRDOS** (AMONG OTHERS) LOOKING OUT FOR YOU. WHICH IS ALMOST **ALWAYS** NICE.

AND YOU MIGHT ACCIDENTALLY TURN YOUR PET GUINEA PIG INTO FIVE PET GUINEA PIGS WHEN YOU MISTAKENLY ZAP THEM WITH A BADDIE'S WONKY LASER GUN . . .

RESULT!!!

And you **might** have noticed I have a NEW **SUPER** **costume**! **FINALLY!** I think **Mum** was so *relieved* that I came back to the *good* side after trying out being a **BADDIE**, she **finally** let me change my costume. It's NOT *exactly* as I wanted it (it was a **hard NO** to the **ROLLER BOOTS** among other things), but I still think it's pretty **COOL** and since my CAPE stopped being **TOO BIG** for me, I really think things have **IMPROVED**.

Most people think that being a **SUPERHERO** is all *WHIZZING* about the **UNIVERSE**, zapping **BADDIES**, striking power poses and bobbing around in a **SPACESHIP**, and they would be *slightly* right. There is a bit of *WHIZZING* and some *ZAPPING* (or glitter storming in my case), but we honestly don't live in a **SPACESHIP** or even a *fancy* futuristic-looking building with lots of glass.

We just live in a very **NORMAL** house, on a **NORMAL** street, in a **NORMAL** town. I do strike the occasional **POWER POSE** but it's not *really* my style, so I just tend to get on with whatever **mission** I have been sent on by **WANDA** . . . she's our pet dog/telephone/pesky tr^{ip}Per-upper. She came to us from **Mission Control**, who are in charge of which **SUPER** goes where, saves what and when, and they let us know via the *soothing sound*** of **WANDA**.

EYE ROLL

24

* Yup, **WANDA**'s sounds are **not** soothing. Not even slightly.

And I don't *just* hang out with **SUPERHEROES**. I hang out with **SUPER BADDIES** too, just don't tell anyone because I am not *really supposed* to. We have got pretty good at being sneaky about it, though, and if I'm *honest*, this **goodie**/**BADDIE** thing isn't always as **clear-cut** as you might think it is.

Not that long ago, KAPOW and Perfecto (my secret **BADDIE** friends) helped save me from going to **THE DARK SIDE** when I got **SUPER** fed up with being a *goodie*. I mean, you would think they would be all for me being a **BADDIE** like them, but they knew it wasn't really me and *helped* me to see that too. I think that's because while they are **SUPER BADDIES**, they are also

SUPER GOOD FRIENDS.

I have **SUPER** good **NORMAL** friends too. Well, they are **not 'NORMAL' normal** – who would want to be **'NORMAL' normal**? But they are *super brilliant* and even when I have found myself in all sorts of **SCRAPES** and got things a bit **WRONG** they have still been the **BEST** friends EVER. *Probably* in the whole history of the **UNIVERSE**. I have my friends from my old school. They are called **Tom** and **Susie** and *unfortunately* these days they are mainly 'on-the-phone friends' but that doesn't stop them being *completely brilliant*.

THE
CHEESE SQUARES

HELP!*

* PLEASE!

Then there are my new school friends . . . they are called **Ivy**, Molly and Ed, and all together we are the school **ECO COUNCIL**. Yes, I know, I can't help myself . . . I just have to save the world wherever I go!!!! We are also in a **BAND** called **The Cheese Squares**, which has so far been completely *underappreciated*, but I am almost *certain* this is only because we are ahead of our time. And speaking of bands, four of my five pet *guinea pigs* are also in a *vocal harmony group* called **THE BERNARDS**. That is because they are all called **BERNARD**. Then there is **STINK-EYE** who is not called **BERNARD** and is also not in the band. This is on account of her being well, **STINKY**. Not in a **SMELLY** way, it's more of a **GRUMPY** vibe. I actually started with just the one *guinea pig* but thanks to a faulty SuperPower Duplicator™ I now have **FIVE**. Anyway, I am almost certain **THE BERNARDS** will be **GLOBAL SUPERSTARS** any day now.

So that's **ME**. **Pizazz**. Age 10 (FINALLY!) A *SUPERHERO!* Ha!

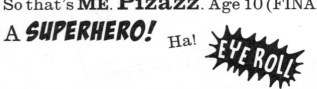

2

The bit where it
starts to go
wrong . . .

It was a **fairly NORMAL** day at school. **NORMAL** if you are a **SUPERHERO**, that is. As usual I had to **ZOOM OFF** during break to **save the world!!!** Well, not quite the world, but a small island as some **slimy alien** overlords had decided (for reasons I am still not sure about) they wanted to rule it and they were NOT asking *nicely.*

The **timing** of this **alien** attack perfectly backed up my theory that while **BADDIES** don't seem to be able to tell the **DIFFERENCE** between night and day (as I am ALWAYS getting **dragged** out of bed to **save the world**), they do seem to know when it is break time and not double maths or **ASSEMBLY** – so **UNFAIR!** Then the **slime** theme continued as I had to eat it (or **lumpy custard** as it is otherwise known) at lunch – UGH!!!! My day got EVEN better as **Serena** decided to be HILARIOUS at afternoon register by very loudly calling me **spacetwit**.

EYE ROLL

Spacetwit? Yes, I know it doesn't make any sense and isn't even *especially* funny, but things like that don't seem to matter when you are the most popular girl in school and have two *sidekicks* – The Populars – to make sure everyone laughs at your fairly RUBBISH jokes. It used to upset me when Serena and The Populars were mean, but while I cannot quite *completely* ignore it yet, I very NEARLY can. This is because I have **VERY SLOWLY** realised that what Serena thinks of me doesn't really matter. SURE, she's popular, but she's not my friend (she very much decided that one) and it's really what friends think that matters. But still . . .

Spacetwit!

EYE ROLL

The rest of the afternoon was pretty *uneventful* (HOORAY!), and I even asked Ivy to come round to my house after school so we could sort out some *important* **ECO COUNCIL** business.

(AGENDA: 1. Set up a **lift-share** system for school drop off.

2. Work out how to **raise money** to set up a **HEDGEHOG HOUSE** in the school grounds.

3. Figure out if we could use all the *hot air* that comes out of *Mr Jones* the PE teacher to heat the gym.)

We were just getting to my front door and deciding what **SNACK** would be best for an **ECO COUNCIL** discussion (we had *narrowed* it down to **toast** with peanut butter or **toast** with jam or maybe even **toast** with peanut butter AND jam), when I *suddenly* found myself **FACE FIRST** in the flower bed.

This could only mean one thing:

WANDA had t**r**ip**p**ed me up . . .

which meant I had a **mission** to go on . . .

which meant Ivy had to go home . . .

which meant NO TOAST with **anything** . . .

EYE ROLL

PIZAZZ STARTS A GLITTER STORM AND POLLUTOOOO STARTS TO SPRAY. BUT THE JAZZ HANDS ARE JUST TOO STRONG AND . . .

THAT IS IT! LAUGH NOW, PIZAZZ, BUT YOU ARE IN FOR A MASSIVE SHOCK. US BADDIES HAVE HAD ENOUGH OF ALL THESE SILLY BATTLES TAKING UP ALL OUR TIME. YOU SEE WE WOULD MUCH RATHER BE . . .

. KNITTING NASTY SCARVES

. . . COOKING NASTY MEALS

MMM, ALIEN TOENAILS AND GORILLA BOGIES.

. . FORMING EVIL PROG ROCK BANDS

. . . ANGRY DANCING

HIGH KICK!

SHOVE!

STAMP!

SO . . .

EVEN LATER . . .

I made it back home in double quick time. I had to warn *everyone* about **TEAM TOXIC**. It sounded super serious, and **Mission Control** needed to know about it **IMMEDIATELY**! When I burst in, **Mum** was building a hover hoover prototype, **Dad** was cooking, **WANDA** was either chewing or **regurgitating** a sock (it was hard to tell which way it was going) and **RED** was breathing/being ANNOYING.

I gathered *everyone* together and then calmly explained everything **POLLUTOOOO** had just told me. **WANDA** put a call through to **Mission Control** straight away and **Aunty Blaze** *WHIZZED* over to check it all out. It felt *good* being in the middle of everything rather than *wondering* what the fuss was about. I was surprised and *extremely* glad that *everyone* seemed to be taking it seriously, that way we could defeat **TEAM TOXIC** immediately and **save Planet Earth**.

HMMMMM, maybe the new *SUPER* **ME** is actually pretty **good** at this!

3

After I had told them *everything* I knew (well, *everything* I knew about **TEAM TOXIC**, not *everything* about *everything*, that would have taken at LEAST another hour), I left **Mum** and **Aunty Blaze** to talk it all over and I went to my room. All this actual **SUPER BUSINESS** was pretty *exhausting*, so I flopped on my bed and imagined all the **SUPERISH** ways I would save the planet from **TEAM TOXIC** . . . I felt almost **EXCITED**, was that **WRONG**?

Then **RED** knocked on my door and as I was in sort of a good mood, I let her come in. Just. She said it was all a bit scary about **TEAM TOXIC** and I said well, yes, but now I had *explained* it all to the grown-ups I was sure it would all be sorted out in no time. Then **Mum** came barging in and told me to be *ready* in five minutes as **Mission Control** needed me to fly in and tell them exactly what **POLLUTOOOO** had said.

OOOOOOOH, fancy!!

I couldn't help but feel slightly *thrilled* as Mum, ~~Aunty Blaze~~ and I zoomed off. I was being a **proper**

SUPER

now.

Everyone **CONGRATULATED** me on a great idea and said maybe I should go home and get some *sleep* while they worked out

the details of that *plan* and I thought that
sounded **fair enough**. I mean, I couldn't
think of everything, could I?

It was **super late** when I got home but I really wanted to see my *spiritual soulmate*, the original BERNARD, for a quick, *reassuring* cuddle. As I neared their hutch, I could hear THE BERNARDS practising for their upcoming **World Tour** and they sounded AMAZING! Their *vocal harmonies* were so completely **AWESOME**, though I suppose it helps when you are all *essentially* the same *guinea pig*. I guess then you know exactly what the others are going to sing **before** they even sing it.

TWOMP!!!

I *apologised* for not being a very good band manager, what with school and **saving the world** taking up so much of my time, but they all smiled and then shoved **Rocket** (**RED**'s *guinea pig*) forward.

Ahhhhh . . . Did this mean she was now THE BERNARDS' band manager? **Yes**. Apparently so. And while I was a bit sad about this, I knew it was for the best. Defeating **TEAM TOXIC** was going to keep me busy and the thought of it all *suddenly* made me feel SUPER tired, so I went to bed.

School was, well, *schoolish* and I was very pleased when the final bell went. It was all very well knowing about **VILLAINOUS GANGS** dead set on destroying the planet, but I was sort of itching to *actually* do something to stop them. It turned out I didn't have to wait long because **WANDA** was waiting for me outside school and she didn't even t^rip me up, just told me I had a **mission** to go on and off I went . . . EYE ROLL

WELL, DUCKS, THAT WIGGLING SCALLYWAG TWERKNADO HAS GOT ON BOARD WITH TEAM TOXIC'S POLLUTING PROGRAMME AN IS BUSY POLLUTING THE CITY WITH NOISE! HIS BANGING BEATS ARE MAKING EVERYON CROSS AND BOTHERED. STOP HIM, PIZAZZ BEFORE THE CITY ERUPTS WITH CROSSNES: AND ALSO BOTHEREDNESS . . .

THE NOISE IS MAKING EVERYONE FURIOUS!!!!

THEY ARE REACHING BOILING POINT

AND TWERKNADO'S POLLUTING IN RHYME . . .

MY LOUD RHYTHMS AND BEATS ARE WINDING UP DA STREE AND MY RAPS AND COOL FL(HAVE GOT EVERYONE READ TO BLOW . . .

I'M GOING TO RAP THIS CITY INTO BITS, THEN I'LL RELEASE MY GREATEST HITS!

It was a blur of **battles** with the **MEANIE** members of **TEAM TOXIC**. We didn't win them all, as *everyone* knows that's *impossible*, but we did convince **MEGAVOM**, **DABOMB**, **VOLTZ** and some others to just stick with their **NORMAL** *BAD BADDINESS* and leave **TEAM TOXIC**. I mean who or what would they threaten with their slime, STINK BOMBS and **SHOCKS** if Planet Earth was actually destroyed?

Slowly but *surely* the **battles** with **TEAM TOXIC** got further and further apart until they seemed to just **STOP**. WHAT? Had we defeated them already? Had we proved just **tooooooo** *SUPER* for them and they had given up?

SORTED!

Take that, **TEAM TOXIC!**

Now I come to think about it, it was a *bit* *optimistic* to think that a few days of **battles** with arch nasties **TEAM TOXIC** would make them run away and give up on **MUCKING** up **the planet** for ever. But *weirdly* that's exactly what we thought. And we were super happy about it. I might have even *suggested* to **Ivy** that we didn't

need to **WORRY** about the **ECO COUNCIL** any more as the **SUPERS** had saved Planet Earth from **DESTRUCTION** once and for all!

UH-OH. I had **no idea** what was coming my way . . .

no idea AT ALL . . . !

Have you ever woken up to one of your best friends talking to you in your head? No? Well, it is very **WEIRD** and sort of **AWESOME** at the same time. I say talking but what *actually* woke me up was **KAPOW** telepathically yelling 'WAKE UP', but once I did, he turned the volume down. A bit.

He explained that **Perfecto** was with him, and she had heard some BIG news about **TEAM TOXIC** from her big sister, **X-tra**, who is a right proper **WRONG 'UN**, **LOVES** being a **BADDIE** and is *apparently* extremely good at it. After all their defeats, **TEAM TOXIC** had decided to recruit some new members and she'd been only too happy to *volunteer*.

And it was **SUPER** easy to get her to spill the beans about all their **DASTARDLY** plans as she was **ITCHING** to show off to Perfecto . . . *Apparently* while us *goodies* had been *WHIZZING* about, high-fiving each other about *defeating* these **NOXIOUS BADDIES**, they had been *regrouping* in their secret **BADDIE** space station and **PLOTTING** a new type of attack.

And according to **KAPOW** that was just the start of it, so . . .

'GET UP AND MEET US ON PLUTO IN TWENTY MINUTES!'

Well now I **WAS** awake.

Ish.

I **didn't** want to go all the way to **PLUTO** on my own at that time of the morning, and I was worried I wouldn't *remember* everything, what with my brain still being 63% asleep . . . so I snuck into **RED**'s room (of course she was *already awake*, dressed and **trimming** her **BONSAI TREES**) to *convince* her to come with me. **Battling** alongside her so much recently had made me sort of *almost* like her. *Slightly*.

I realised I hadn't probably ever really been in her room before as I was usually telling her to **GET OUT** of mine. It was actually *quite nice*, even if it was a **BIT TOOOO NEAT**, the sort of **NEAT** that makes you feel **uncomfortable** because even just by *breathing* you feel like you are messing it up. I told her we HAD to go to **PLUTO** on top-secret **TEAM TOXIC**

business. **R ED** didn't even stop her **pruning** as she asked me why we had to go when it was obviously all sorted . . . didn't I *remember* we had **saved the day???** I explained that maybe we hadn't, and we HAD to go to **PLUTO** to meet some people who had some *information* that might be helpful.

Then **R ED** did stop **pruning** and asked who we had to meet and why couldn't **Mission Control** go? I said that we didn't have time for all that now and we should just GO. Then she looked at me all **funny** and said she wasn't going ANYWHERE until I told her who was on **PLUTO** and I was starting to **REALLY REGRET** asking her to come with me, but it was *too late now* so I made her **SWEAR** on her copy of **BONSAI TREE WEEKLY** that she wouldn't tell, and only when she had done that did I spill the beans that we were off to meet my two **SECRET BADDIE** friends . . .

BONSAI TREE WEEKLY

RED sort of gasped, went a bit Wibbly and *accidentally* cut a **BONSAI TREE** in half, but I explained that there was **NO TIME** for Wibbling, and that she should *trust me*, because I *trusted them*, and they hadn't let me down yet. **RED** *argued* that we should tell the **grown-ups** and let them deal with it. I *pointed* out we should probably NOT do that as these were my ***SECRET BADDIE FRIENDS*** and as they were already breaking the ***BADDIE CODE*** to help us, I didn't want to get them into **TROUBLE**.

I also *pointed* out that **Mum** probably hadn't had her coffee yet so would not react well

to ANYTHING, let alone THIS. And then I *pointed* out that if we got the full story first, she might get *WHIZZED* off to **Mission Control** this time to tell them all about it. I could see **RED** warming to this idea. Then I finally *pointed* out that maybe we should bring **JETT**, **PINK GIRL** and CHAMELEON along too – it sort of felt like we were a bit of a **SUPER GANG** after all we had just been through – and **RED** sprang into action, sneaking downstairs to call and tell them all to meet us on **PLUTO** in fifteen minutes – NO QUESTIONS – while I stopped *pointing* and started getting ready.

BUT THEN ...

KAPOW and Perfecto were already there when we arrived on PLUTO and so was JETT, but she was standing about fifty metres away from them looking a bit **cross**. She *immediately* called me over to ask if I was dabbling in **THE DARK SIDE** again and what was I doing making her meet some *BADDIES* before she'd even had her **CHEERY FLAKES**? I told her that no, I was still a *goodie* (pretty much), and that KAPOW and Perfecto were not only my actual friends, but when it came to **TEAM TOXIC**, they were on our side.

I could see JETT wasn't at all sure about this, then RED's *SUPER BUDDIES* turned up and they looked like they weren't at all sure about it either. The awkward *frostiness* was making me itchy and I realised I had to sort this out asap. But HOW??? Then I *remembered* I had, erm, *borrowed* some packets of **prawn cocktail** crisps (is there any other flavour?) from the **SNACK** cupboard as we *WHIZZED* out of the kitchen and shoved them in the pockets of my new **CAPE** ... yes, you heard that right ... **POCKETS!!!** And yes, I am a fashion genius and once all the *SUPERS* see my **CAPE POCKETS** they will realise this and want them too. Anyway, what brings people together better than **crisps**, huh? Or **CAPE** pockets? Yup, nothing. So, I opened the crisps to share them out. *Unfortunately*, what with **PLUTO** not having much in the way of gravity, the crisps floated away immediately. As some of us can fly (soz, **RED**) we managed to catch a few, but most of them got away – you are welcome, space mice (What? You didn't know?) and while it was quite *heartbreaking* to see my favourite **SNACK** drifting off into **OUTER SPACE**, I couldn't mind too much as the chilly atmosphere had slightly warmed up (not actually on **PLUTO**, where it's -387 degrees, but the chilly *goodie*/*BADDIE* atmosphere).

Is there anything **crisps** cannot do?

After I explained to *everyone* that **KAPOW** and **Perfecto** were taking a huge risk by meeting us and would get in super **BIG TROUBLE** if their parents found out, everyone agreed to listen. Then **KAPOW** and **Perfecto** quickly spilled everything they knew, which in **KAPOW**'s case wasn't that much as he didn't have an **EVIL** big sister, which felt like both a *good* and a *BAD* thing in this *particular* situation. But **Perfecto** had loads of information as her sister **LOVED** showing off everything she knew about **TEAM TOXIC**.

And **Perfecto** being **Perfecto** had put it all in a **colour-coded**, **cross-referenced binder**. Obviously. It was so super **NEAT** and **TIDY**, **RED** actually **SQUEALED** when she saw it. Even I had to admit it was some *excellent* stationery work.

Then **Perfecto** looked a bit sad because she isn't ever so keen on being a ***BADDIE***, and so sort of knows she will **never** be as *good* at it as her sister. I wanted to tell her that I knew **exactly** what that was like (except with *goodyness*) and that what she really needed to do was to find her own way to being a ***PROPER ROTTER***, but there wasn't time for that now and there was **NO WAY** I was going to say it in front of **RED**. So instead, I put my arm around **Perfecto** in a way I hoped was *reassuring* and she told us what she knew . . .

Perfecto looked like she might **cry** the whole time she was telling us about **TEAM TOXIC**'s plan and I felt *extremely* awful for her. According to her sister, **TEAM TOXIC** had *realised* that **NORMAL battles** were not working fast enough and they were wasting time losing too many of them. SO, they had *decided* that instead of them **MESSING** up Planet Earth they would get the people that lived there to do it *instead*.

Well, I had to laugh at this because

WHO WOULD DO THAT?

Muck up the very planet they live on?

PAH!

Then **Perfecto** carried on and *explained* that **TEAM TOXIC** had realised that what with all the **POLLUTION**, damage to the **ENVIRONMENT** and **RUBBISH**, the people on Earth were sort of **MUCKING** things up already. So, their **plan** was to just speed things up a bit by *encouraging* people to keep doing what they were ALREADY doing, just a bit **more**. Then I stopped *laughing*. Uh-oh.

This was in fact a **brilliant plan.**

I thought about all the **UNRECYCLED JUICE CARTONS** in the canteen **RUBBISH BINS**, the paper in the **WASTE BIN** in class and the **LITTER** people left in Gramps's park. Then I remembered Serena's dad, Mr Piffle, and his **strange** need to try and turn *everything* into money and I did a little shiver.

Yes, this was a **brilliant plan**, but we HAD to DEFEAT it. ALL we had to do was think of a *slightly* **MORE brilliant plan** ...

SOME TIME LATER . . .

I had to admit we were a bit stuck. None of us **SUPERS** were used to **battling** this way, we were more used to *ZAPPING* and *WHIZZING* and glitter storming. It was clear we might need bit of *help* and should *probably* tell our grown-ups – but **how** could we explain where we got all our info from?

Spying space mice? *Accidentally* finding Perfecto's **binder** on a space bus? An **ANONYMOUS SUPER SOURCE?**

We all agreed that an **ANONYMOUS SUPER SOURCE** was probably the best bet, and we all swore not to *reveal* it as the grown-ups were bound to ask.

And then ask **again**.

And then ask **again**.

And *possibly* ask **a few times more**.

We all **zoomed** back to our houses to get ready for *school* and have breakfast and of course tell our **parents** about **TEAM TOXIC**'s genius plan . . . It went **really** well . . .

. . . NOT!

NO WAY . . .

We were *shocked*. Even **more** shocked than the time RED **forgot** to do her homework . . . the grown-ups were basically *ignoring* us. It was like they didn't want to hear anything we had to say. I knew these weren't the **NORMAL battles** us *SUPERS* fought, but if me, RED, JETT, **PINK GIRL**, CHAMELEON, **KAPOW** AND Perfecto could see how big a threat this was, why on **EARTH**, **MARS** or even **JUPITER** couldn't the grown-ups? Just because **POLLUTION** doesn't have a *LASER GUN*, and **CLIMATE CHANGE** doesn't look like a cross between an **OCTOPUS**, a **VAMPIRE** and **LUMPY CUSTARD**, and **RUBBISH** doesn't have an **EVIL** laugh, didn't mean they were any less **BAD**. Why didn't the grown-ups get it?

We even tried to convince **WANDA** . . .

. . . but that didn't work either.

Did this mean we would have to deal with this on our own? ***GULP***

90

5

The bit where Team Toxic GO, GO, GO . . .

I MUST BE A PROPER BUSINESS PERSON NOW I HAVE A BRIEF CASE!

BOWLER HAT!

I AM AN ACTUAL EXECUTIVE BECAUSE I HAVE EXECUTIVE DESK TOYS . . . SEE?

THEIR FANCY NEW OFFICES, TOXICO (AS THEY ARE NOW OWN) GET BUSY BRAINSTORMING LOTS OF HORRIBLE YS TO MUCK UP PLANET EARTH, BUT, YOU KNOW, AN ACCEPTABLE WAY . . .

LESS NATURE?

THEN LET'S LIE ABOUT ALL OF IT!

MORE FOSSIL FUELS?

MORE PLASTIC?

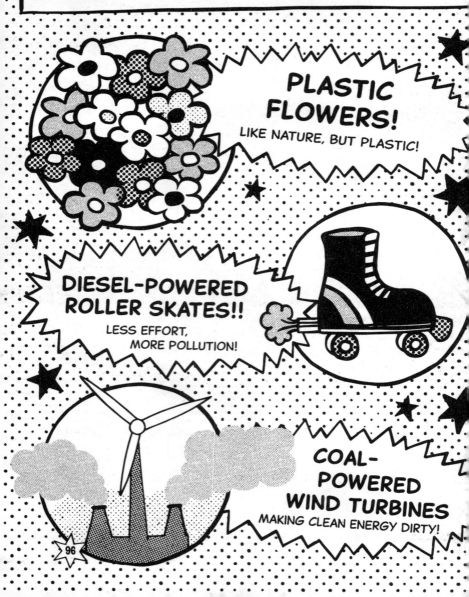

SOME TIME LATER . . .

We were all pretty *exhausted*, what with **NORMAL missions**, trying to defeat **TEAM TOXIC** AND go to school and I *think* it was starting to show.

Mum even had the cheek to ask us what was **WRONG**, which was a BIT MUCH . . . so I tried to explain all about **ToxiCo** to her and **Dad** AGAIN. But this time I also told them that while it was up to them if they *believed* us or not, or even **helped** us or not, it was not up to them whether we kept trying to do something about it or not. I told her that even though NONE of the grown-up **SUPERS** seemed to think it was important, WE knew it was and we were going to do everything we could to stop it.

Then I smiled at **RED** and *amazingly* THAT was the bit that tipped **Mum** over the edge and she *demanded* to know what was going on and so I told her . . . we are **SAVING THE WORLD**.

It seemed a bit odd that after ALL the times Mum has told me to be a more *enthusiastic* **SUPER**, when I told her I was *spontaneously* **saving the planet** she TOLD ME OFF.

Apparently **saving the world** was only a good idea if you did it when **Mission Control** told you to. I asked what you did when **Mission Control** was ignoring the planet being properly **MUCKED UP** right under its nose even though a bunch of *highly intelligent* and *extremely cool* kids were repeatedly telling them. It turns out you '**GO TO YOUR ROOM**'.

I slumped into the classroom realising this **mission** was going to be super **TRICKY**, possibly the **TRICKIEST** I had ever faced. Somehow, thanks to **TEAM TOXIC** AKA **ToxiCo**'s **brilliant** plan, we were stuck **battling** the very people we were trying to protect. Our **SUPER POWERS** didn't seem to be much use with these types of **battles** and *anyway*, lots of people seemed to *actually* like the things that **TEAM TOXIC** AKA **ToxiCo** were doing and selling, even if they hurt the planet. It was all so **befuddling**, and my face must have been **befuddled** too as Molly asked if I was OK. But before I could **unfuddle** my thoughts and answer, we were *interrupted* by **Serena** on the other side of the classroom telling everyone VERY LOUDLY how **EXCITING** it was that her **dad**, **Mr Piffle**, was going to be on the TV later.

Apparently, he was the newest member of an **INTERGALACTIC** group dedicated to something or other **BIG-BUSINESS**-related and he wanted to let everyone know that this **BIG BUSINESS** wanted the best for *everyone* and part of that was giving *everyone* the *opportunity* to buy their very own *Handy Hands*™, made from 100% unrecycled plastic. **THE NEW SENSATION SWEEPING THE NATION** brought to you by . . . My chin hit the floor, I felt all Wibbly and then I caught **JETT**'s eye . . . It couldn't be, could it? We zoomed over to where *Serena* was waffling on, just in time to hear her say **TOXICO**!

103

...OOOOOOOOOOO!

Well, this was a new twist . . . **TEAM TOXIC** AKA **ToxiCo** had obviously *branched* out and had now recruited a **NORMAL BADDIE** to help with their **EVIL PLANS** . . . **Mr Piffle** and his **BIG BUSINESS**. I REALLY couldn't figure out why someone who actually *lived* on this **planet** would play such a big part in its **downfall**. But I would have to work that out later, right now we had to figure out how to stop them.

Everyone was *gathering* around **Serena** and listening to all the nonsense she was telling them about **TEAM TOXIC** AKA **ToxiCo** and their *Handy Hands*™. I felt all **HOT** and before I knew it, I had flown over and told **Serena** that **ToxiCo** were actually a group of **EVIL SUPER BADDIES** called **TEAM TOXIC** and they were all set on really, REALLY **MUCKING** up **Planet Earth** and they were just using her **dad** and his **BIG BUSINESS** to help **pollute** the environment so they could achieve their **DASTARDLY** aim. And *anyway*, we all had hands already, why did we need plastic ones?

Then I stopped because I felt almost certain that was more than enough *information* and surely she had to see my point. But it wasn't and she didn't. She just looked at me like I had **TWO HEADS** (not four hands as apparently that was now the minimum), then laughed her **EVIL LAUGH**, told me to **CHILL OUT** and stop being such a misery and that maybe I needed a *Handy Hand*™ to cheer me up. Well, that did it. MY actual hands started twitching and I could feel a jazz hands/ glitter storm (still *biodegradable*, OBVS!) coming on and I wasn't sure I was able to stop it . . .

MWA HA HA!

Why couldn't **Serena** see that what her **dad** was doing was properly ***BAD*** for the planet and her actual future? And why was she helping him? I was so **UPSET** I didn't think I could hold in the glitter storm much longer when suddenly **JETT** *WHIZZED* in and **SHOVED** me back to my seat on the other side of the classroom. She told me to **CALM DOWN** and that we would sort all of this out – just not this way – then she *hovered* back to her desk. I knew she was right but

AGGGHHHHHH^HH!

I was still feeling very it $c\,\mathfrak{h}\mathfrak{y}$ about it all when Ivy came into class looking **SUPER HAPPY**. It turned out that the school **pond** we had been trying to save for aaaaages was now **officially** saved, thanks to her *creature* count. Basically, Ivy had sat by the **pond** all day counting up all the *different species* of *animals* and *insects* that visited the **pond** and there were so many (and one of them was a **bit rare**) that it couldn't be filled in to make more car parking spaces after all. Ivy had done it, AGAIN!

Then Ed arrived and heard the good news, and we were all very busy *congratulating* Ivy when I suddenly realised . . . OF COURSE!!! **SUPER POWERS** weren't going to win this **battle**, Ivy powers were. **THE ECO COUNCIL** powers were. Protecting the planet and trying to get people to *understand* that they should too was what Ivy and the rest of us **ECOCOUNCILLORS** did all the time. We had stood up to **Mr Piffle** before and now we had to do it again (even if he was now backed by an **INTERGALACTIC** band of *NASTIES*). These were the powers that were going to save us. Well, and the occasional biodegradable glitter storm, but MAINLY Ivy powers!!!!

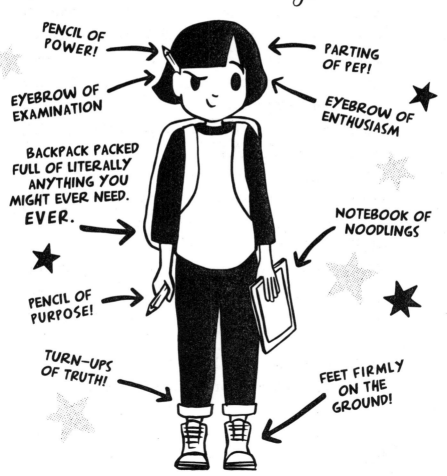

PENCIL OF POWER!

PARTING OF PEP!

EYEBROW OF EXAMINATION

EYEBROW OF ENTHUSIASM

BACKPACK PACKED FULL OF LITERALLY ANYTHING YOU MIGHT EVER NEED. EVER.

NOTEBOOK OF NOODLINGS

PENCIL OF PURPOSE!

TURN-UPS OF TRUTH!

FEET FIRMLY ON THE GROUND!

There was no time to lose . . . I called **JETT** back over so I wouldn't have to say it twice – I was **saving energy** already! – and explained it all as *calmly* as I could. I mean, I didn't want to scare **Ivy**, Molly and Ed too much, what with them not being as used to **CERTAIN PERIL** as I am. I think they all took it really well . . .

When I finished, **Ivy** raised an eyebrow and asked what had happened to the **SUPERS** having the whole **planet-saving** thing licked? And I just looked at my shoes and *mumbled* that I might have got that a bit **WRONG**. Then, in the *brilliant* way that **Ivy** does, she forgot all about that and started planning. We agreed it was hard to know exactly what **EVIL** attempts to **DESTROY** the environment were down to **TEAM TOXIC** and what was just the **NORMAL** everyday stuff, so **Ivy** said we had to defeat them all . . . Oh. OK, then.

But maybe we should start with the **Handy Hands**™ . . .

Then **Mrs Harris** came in to take the register and *interrupted* our *plotting*, so we agreed to meet up after school to come up with a proper plan. I suggested our usual meeting place of **PLUTO**, but **JETT** pointed out that the sub-zero temperatures and lack of gravity might prove a bit of a *challenge* for the **NORMALS**, so we decided on the end of my garden, behind the shed. I was a little bit **cross** about having to wait so long to get started as I was sure **TEAM TOXIC** AKA **ToxiCo** didn't have to worry about going to school during their **DASTARDLY** scheming – *SO UNFAIR.*

JETT would come via **KAPOW** and **Perfecto**'s houses later, and I planned to **sneak** a message to **RED** at *lunchtime* telling her to round up her friends and get them there too.

Then **Mrs Harris** told us all to STOP TALKING so we did.

And while I knew we had SO MUCH to do if we were to have any hope of beating **TEAM TOXIC** AKA **ToxiCo**, now **Ivy** had her thinking face on things already felt a bit better.

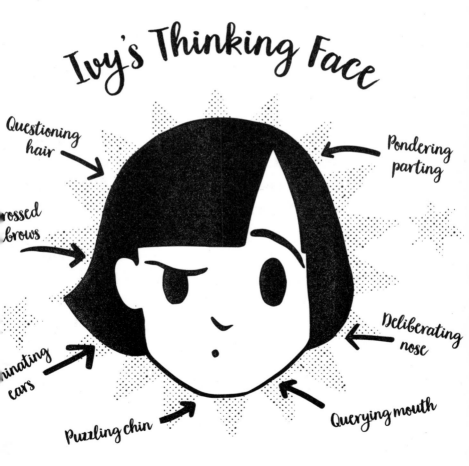

Ivy's Thinking Face

Questioning hair

Pondering parting

rossed brows

Deliberating nose

inating ears

Puzzling chin

Querying mouth

The school day really *dragged* on, *probably* because I was BURSTING to get home for our meeting. It felt like there was **no time to lose** and it was hard not to yell that at *everyone* all day, but even I realised that wouldn't help anything.

As soon as I got home, I *immediately* went behind the shed in the garden so I would be there first. Well, when I say immediately what I mean is that I made a **SNACK** first. *Obviously* I couldn't **concentrate** on defeating an entire **EVIL SUPER SQUAD** if I was hungry, could I?

Then I thought that everyone else might be hungry too and as I REALLY needed them to be able to *concentrate*, I had to get even more **SNACKS**. And then I had to check they all tasted nice.

Then **Mum** came in and asked me what I was doing, and I told her quite *matter-of-factly* that I was 'Getting **SNACKS**' and walked *purposefully* out into the garden with as much as I could carry.

Amazingly she didn't come after me. Sometimes it's just about *confidence*.

By the time I had carried ALL the **SNACKS** ALL the way to *almost* the bottom of the garden, **JETT**, Perfecto and **KAPOW** had already arrived. **RED** was there too, with her **SUPER-KEEN SUPER FRIENDS** and **Milly Martin**, the *only* person in **RED**'s class who has more monitor ribbons than her. Then **Ivy** and Molly turned up, but of course Ed was late. We decided to start without Ed because you could never *really* be sure when he would arrive and we knew he wouldn't *really* mind.

After we had a very *passionate* discussion about whether or not we should have **badges**

(conclusion – yes, but only paper ones), we decided what we should be called. This took quite a while, but we were all very *pleased* when we ended up with **Supers And Normals Determinedly Working In Cahoots Helping Earth Survive**. Or **S.A.N.D.W.I.C.H.E.S.** for short. I mean who doesn't like sandwiches? Ed arrived and said he *definitely* did, so that decided it!

THEN **Perfecto** mentioned that she had got even more *information* from her **BIG BAD** sister, X-tra . . .

6

The bit where we put our heads together . . .

Perfecto then told us that the word around **TEAM TOXIC** AKA **ToxiCo** was that their plan was a success. Obviously it was only early days but their **TRICKSTER ADVERTS** were working already, and people seemed to be actually *believing* their nonsense. Yes, the total stinkers in **TEAM TOXIC** AKA **ToxiCo** were all very pleased that the people of Planet Earth were buying into all their nonsense and **POLLUTING** the planet even more than they were before.

And they were *particularly* pleased as people were buying as many *Handy Hands*™, the new *sensation* sweeping the nation, as they could get their, erm, hands on. Which turned out to be A LOT, what with all the extra hands they now had. **Perfecto** said her sister had even been *bragging* about how **TOTALLY TOXIC** they were . . .

HOW TO MAKE SOME
Handy Hands™

Yay! Woo!

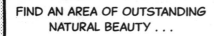

FIND AN AREA OF OUTSTANDING NATURAL BEAUTY . . .

. . . GET RID OF ALL THE OUTSTANDING NATURAL BEAUTY . .

DRILL FOR OIL . . .

. . . TRY AGAIN . . .

. . . AND AGAIN . . .

FIND SOME OIL AND EXTRACT IT . . .

. . . TAKE THE OIL TO THE LAB IN A STINKY LORRY. . .

. . . SEPARATE OIL INTO LIQUIDS AND GASES USING POWER GENERATED BY LOTS OF CUTE, BUT SAD, HAMSTERS.*

NOW YOU HAVE MADE PLASTIC!

THEN FIND ANOTHER LOVELY SPOT, THIS TIME BY A RIVER . . .

HEN MAKE IT UNLOVELY BY UILDING A BIG HAND-MAKING ACTORY THERE . . .

STAFF IT WITH EVIL ROBOTS

HEN PRESS START . . . GIVE YOURSELF A HAND!

USE MORE PAPER AND PLASTIC TO PACKAGE YOUR HANDY HANDS.

We were all super shocked. We knew it had been going well for **TEAM TOXIC** AKA **ToxiCo**, but we were all still a bit shocked their plan was working SO easily – much easier than **battling BADDIES** all the time. Everyone just believed everything **TEAM TOXIC** AKA **ToxiCo** spewed out, without questioning it. We didn't *understand* why no one seemed *interested* in the truth. Even if that truth was a bit scary, at least it was the ACTUAL truth and then once you knew it you could sort it out.

Ivy said that she didn't think it was that simple and that sometimes people just wanted to believe *everything* is OK rather than to admit it isn't and actually have to do *something* about it. Then she pointed out that we had been TRYING to convince our parents (who were actual **SUPERS** whose **actual job** it is to save the **actual planet**) that TEAM TOXIC AKA ToxiCo were putting the **Earth** in danger, and even they wouldn't listen. Ugh. It was so *frustrating*, but I knew I couldn't get cross now, we had too much to do.

We all agreed that jazz hands/glitter storms (even biodegradable ones) weren't going to help us here, or **super speedy, jet-propelled**

SUPERHEROES

or even **FIRE-BREATHING** little sisters. What we *actually* had to do was to convince people to listen to the **TRUTH** and stop buying *Handy Hands™*. BUT HOW?

That's when **Ivy** rolled up her sleeves and said we had to take **ACTION** and we all got very **EXCITED** about this until we realised that right then the only action we had to take was to go home for tea. **EYE ROLL** But **Ivy** said she would work on a plan and we could talk about it *tomorrow* at school, and **KAPOW** would listen in with his telepathic powers and tell **Perfecto**, **PINK GIRL** and CHAMELEON about it.

After everyone had gone home, I went to my room but I couldn't sit still, which was **VERY** unusual. I felt all WRIGGLY. I was used to the good vs **EVIL battles** that **WANDA** sent me on, where I would use my special powers to win or lose and that was that, done and dusted (or even glittered!) But this felt so complicated and so much bigger than that.

Probably because it was . . . *hundreds*, maybe even *thousands*, possibly even *millions* of little **battles** we would have to fight . . . *sometimes* with our choices, sometimes with our actions and *sometimes* with our **SUPER POWERS**. If I was honest, it felt like A LOT, but I couldn't let that put me off, I just had to get on with it,

one

battle

at a

TIME.

I used some of my extra WRIGGLY energy to go see THE BERNARDS. They were having one last practice before their **World Tour**. I couldn't *believe* how far they had come and was super EXCITED for the adventure they were about to have, but also a bit sad I wasn't going on it with them. BERNARD THE FIRST came over for a cuddle, and then I stopped being sad and started being really happy for her and the other BERNARDS.

Rocket seemed to have *everything* under control for the **Tour** and I was so **relieved** as I was certain I wouldn't have been even half as good as a band manager. Reassuringly STINK-EYE was still giving VERY STINKY EYE from the corner of the hutch . . . all was as it should be.

Then **Mum** called me for tea, and I was feeling PRETTY PECKISH until I saw **Mr Piffle** on the TV in the kitchen . . .

7

The bit where we work
out what to do . . .

Then do it . . .

RED and I met JETT, MILLY, Ivy, Molly and Ed in the playground before school the next day. Everyone had seen Mr Piffle's bit on TV the night before and were now looking VERY serious. Well, *everyone* except Ed but I think that's just not how his face works.

KAPOW let me know he was **listening** in (I just had to remember to '*think*' the whole *conversation*!) and then we started . . . Ivy said that from what she could work out from all the ads, posters and information TEAM TOXIC AKA ToxiCo were *bombarding* everyone with, the way to beat them would be to do all the things we had been doing as the ECO COUNCIL but just MUCH, MUCH BIGGER . . . YES!

Of course, I mean it was *obvious* really. But, erm, **how**?

We *decided* to start after school in the park . . .

Then we got **Gramps** to take us to the *supermarket* so we could try there . . .

Then we ALL **tried** when we got home . . .

AGAIN . . .

I couldn't *understand* it, why was no one listening to us? It wasn't fair . . . we were trying to **protect** our **planet**, our **future**, and no one was *listening*. Was it just because we were kids? Was it because

these **battles** weren't the usual *WHIZZY* ones? How were we going to stop this? Were **TEAM TOXIC** AKA **ToxiCo** going to win? And so easily? It was like we were the only ones who cared . . .

THIS IS **NOT** OK!

I practically *slithered* into school, I felt so hopeless about it all. **TEAM TOXIC** AKA **ToxiCo** were pumping out LIES, **POLLUTION** and plastic things **faster** and **faster** and we didn't seem to be getting anywhere. **EYE ROLL**

But when I got to class **Ivy** was there and practically bouncing off the walls with joyfulness. Er, *hello?* Had she completely forgotten about the day before when we completely **FAILED** to save the planet? Had she missed **Mr Piffle** on the telly two nights ago?

It turned out she hadn't, but she HAD realised **S.A.N.D.W.I.C.H.E.S.** might have to rethink our tactics. Apparently, we had started at the **WRONG** end. Er, what? **Ivy** explained that maybe we should be talking to people like us, people who got it . . . KIDS! Telling **our** friends and getting **them** to tell **their** friends and getting **them** to tell **THEIR** friends and getting **them** to tell **their**

friends and, well, you get the idea.

She pointed out that us kids were very GOOD at that sort of thing, just look at the **shoelace CRAZE**! And that time everyone HAD to have a *JOLLY GOOD* **sticker**. And when we all went mad for COLLECTING **conkers**. And then there was the most recent example . . . *Handy Hands™*, the new *sensation* sweeping the nation. And maybe that's where we should start. We would start a rival craze to *Handy Hands™*, an even NEWER *sensation* that would sweep the nation. Just our one WOULDN'T have toys or **stuff**. Our craze was not the *Handy Hands™* craze it was the **HANDS OFF OUR FUTURE** craze. Our craze would make a **DIFFERENCE**, a **GOOD DIFFERENCE**.

Perfect. O. LOL.

Well, this all made *perfect* sense and we decided to start **RIGHT AWAY**. We made flyers at break time and the nice man in the library *photocopied* them for us. We included a **comic strip** of all the awful things that happened just to make one pair of *Handy Hands™*. I can't remember whose idea that was.

Then we hit the *playground* at lunch to hand them out. And while **not** everyone wanted to hear what we had to say, *lots* did and even asked us **questions** about it. Some of the teachers asked us about the flyers too and we were all thinking we might just be able to do this, make our **craze** out-craze *Handy Hands™* . . . until we went into class and **Mrs Harris** asked us to stay back after afternoon register to talk about a leaflet she had found in the *playground* . . .

As we sat watching *everyone* else leave for P.E., **Serena** made a big point of waving 'bye bye' to us with her **Handy Hands**™ and **LAUGHING**. UGH! It was so *unfair*, we were trying our best to defeat an **INTERGALACTIC** bunch of **NASTIES**,

determined to **MUCK** up the planet for EVERYONE, and WE were the ones in trouble? I felt Wobbly and **furious** all at the **same time** and I was trying to pick just one thing to feel when Mrs Harris sat down in front of us . . .

gulp

We all nodded our heads, braced for a telling-off. Then something completely weird and AMAZING happened . . . we **didn't** get told off!!!

In fact, Mrs Harris said that we had **actually** done a *good* thing and she was **happy** to see we were so *passionate* about looking after the planet. She said the **ECO COUNCIL** had challenged some *important* issues in the past and she was **pleased** to see we were branching out (maybe pun intended, it was hard to tell) into things outside of school.

She even said she had learned a thing or two from our flyers. Then she said the best thing of all . . . that she had decided to do all she could to *support* **saving the planet** in school and she would even speak to the **HEAD TEACHER** about it. Finally, she said that we should do an **ASSEMBLY** about **S.A.N.D.W.I.C.H.E.S.** Not the ones you eat, though – US!

Well, we weren't expecting that.

The bell went for the end of school, and we all walked out into the busy *playground* in a bit of a *daze*. What a day . . .

We were so *dazed* it took us a little bit of time to **realise** the playground felt a bit busier than usual, but once we did, we saw that loads of kids were handing the leaflets we had made to their grown-ups and telling them about S.A.N.D.W.I.C.H.E.S. Some of the grown-ups looked a bit **cross** and some a bit CONFUSED, but lots were actually listening.

We allowed ourselves to feel a bit EXCITED.

The **HANDS OFF OUR FUTURE** craze was

GO!

I told **R FD** about what **Mrs Harris** had said on the way home and she *promised* to pass it on to **Milly**, **PINK GIRL** and CHAMELEON — she was sure they would come for the **ASSEMBLY**. Then we BOTH fell *through* the front door. **WANDA**! Of course!

But it was usually just me flat out on the hall floor and it made a change to be **tripped** up with **R FD**, and I was sort of thinking it felt nice to do more things together.

WEIRD!

Then I *allowed* myself to be dragged into the kitchen for a briefing by **WANDA** for a **mission** we all had to go on . . .

HEROES TRY TO CONFRONT SEPTIC SQUIRREL . . .

BUT HE DOESN'T SEEM TO NOTICE THEM. OR MAYBE HE CAN'T HEAR THEM . . . ?

SO THEY ALL YELLED AT THE

TOP OF THEIR LUNGS . . .

T THAT DIDN'T SEEM TO WORK EITHER . . .

AT SHOULD OUR HEROES DO NOW?

ALL THE THINKING HAS MADE DAD PECKISH . . .

RUSTLE!
RUSTLE!
RUSTLE!

NUTS!

. . . AND IT SEEMS THAT SEPTIC SQUIRREL CAN HEAR A BAG OF NUTS OPENING OVER THE SOUND OF A CHAINSAW!!!

EN DAD HAS AN IDEA . . . MELTS INTO A CAGE . . .

. . . WHILE MUM LEAVES A TRAIL OF CHILLI NUTS . . .

SEPTIC SQUIRREL IS POWERLESS TO RESIST THE DELICIOUS NUTTY GOODNESS . . .

SLAM!!

When we got home, **RED** and I walked into the kitchen *braced* for our telling-off. Maybe **Mum** and **Dad** had found about **S.A.N.D.W.I.C.H.E.S.** and maybe they weren't *keen*. Not about the ones you **eat**, though. We all know *everyone* likes those.

I was just getting ready to defend *our* **S.A.N.D.W.I.C.H.E.S.** when **Mum** said '**sorry**'. Er, what now? Had I heard that *correctly*? Or was this another symptom of being hit over the head with a **LLAMA** (still a long story)? Then she said it

again and after I checked with **R ED** that she really had *actually* said **sorry**, I was so shocked I just fell over. Once I had got up again, she said that **Mrs Harris** had *called* to *congratulate* her on having two kids that cared about the **planet** so much. And then **Mrs Harris** had told her about our *leaflet* and upcoming **ASSEMBLY**. **Mum** said that she was sorry she hadn't listened properly and that *sometimes* **grown-ups** forget that kids can know stuff that they don't. And then she said we should tell *everyone* all about it.

So we did . . .

Then *everyone* suggested ways they could **help** . . .

Then we *reminded* them of what WE HAD JUST TOLD THEM . . .

. . . and they came up with some more suggestions . . .

It felt good *convincing* my family to make some changes, *teaching* them how to **save the planet** in new and, well, if I am totally honest, less EXCITING ways. But while they might be less whizzy, KAPOWY and EXCITING, they were still super important, in fact if *anything* they were **more important**. And RED reminded everyone that now they knew about it, they had to tell *everyone* else about our new craze!

Remembering about the LLAMAS reminded me they owed me one (you know, what with the *head hitting*). Maybe they could help us, I mean it was their **planet** too. So, before tea, RED and I *decided* to go and ask for their help . . .

HELLOOOOO?

HEY, LLAMAS, WE NEED YOUR HELP . . .

THEN SUDDENLY . . .

WHY SHOULD WE?

PIZAZZ BRAVELY STARTS TO TALK . . .

REMEMBER ME? IT'S A LONG STORY BUT HERE GOES . .

HE LLAMAS LISTEN . . .

. . . AND YOU HIT ME ON THE HEAD!

AND THEN PIZAZZ FINISHES WITH . . .

. . . THE BIG EYES!

Ok

FINE.

GREAT!!! ALL WE NEED YOU TO DO IS . . .

QUITE A LONG WHILE LATER . . .

. . . AND SAVE PLANET EARTH!!!

IS THAT ALL

SURE.

THE LLAMAS WASTED NO TIME . . .

It felt good having *nature* on our side –
well, some of it anyway. R**E**D and I were
super **EXCITED** when we told the rest of the
S.A.N.D.W.I.C.H.E.S. at our meeting after
tea. We did this one on the computer as now
everyone's parents knew about us, we didn't
have to be so *sneaky*. That meant that **Susie**
and **Tom** could join in too, and they could start
making their own **S.A.N.D.W.I.C.H.E.S.**
back in my old school.

And then things got even better when
Molly told us the **ASSEMBLY** was going
to be in three days and **Ivy** said she was
almost positive she had *convinced* the
local paper to come along. It really felt like
we were getting *somewhere* and maybe that
somewhere was a **GOOD PLACE!**
What could go WRONG?

IN AN ATTEMPT TO APPEAR EVEN MORE ACCEPTABLE, TOXICO HAVE A VOTE TO DECIDE WHO SHOULD
HEIR SPOKESPERSON, THE FRIENDLY FACE OF TOXICO . . . WHAT ABOUT PLASTICO FANTASTICO . . . ?
AIN NOTVERYNICE . . . ?
TIC SQUIRREL . . . ?
PIFFLE . . . ?
MR PIFFLE IT IS!

AND MR PIFFLE WASTED NO TIME IN BEING, WELL, ACCEPTABLE . . .

HE HUGGED CUTE KITTENS . . .

HE HUGGED BABIES . . .

HE HUGGED OLD LADIES . . .

WHETHER THEY WANTED HIM TO OR NOT (MAINLY NOT)! MEANWHILE, TOXICO WERE MAKING SURE THEIR DASTARDLY PLAN WAS STILL IN ACTION . . .

Ivy had arranged for the **S.A.N.D.W.I.C.H.E.S.** to meet in the hall after school to practise our **ASSEMBLY**, though you could tell that we were all struggling to be *enthusiastic*, what with all the stuff that **TEAM TOXIC** AKA ToxiCo and **Mr Piffle** were doing. It felt like no matter how hard we tried and how much truth we told, some people just didn't want to change.

We had decided to do a song as **The Cheese Squares** (the group we formed for the school talent show) as part of our **ASSEMBLY**, but with the rest of the **S.A.N.D.W.I.C.H.E.S.** joining in too. Like a super group . . . **Cheese S.A.N.D.W.I.C.H.E.S.** Ed was practising his **maracas** solo when the hall doors flung open and the most *surprising* thing of all happened. Well, possibly not the **most** *surprising* thing of all – that would have been the **HEAD TEACHER** walking in on her **hands** balancing a box of ice pops for everyone on her right **foot**. Or *something*.

BUT it was still really surprising when **Serena** and **The Populars** walked in.

Serena had our leaflet in her hand and asked us if it was, like, true and we said it really was. And then she asked if, like, **ToxiCo** properly **MUCK** up **the planet** then does that mean 'I can't wear my new coat?', 'Or have ever-so-lovely hair?', 'Or, like, go shopping?' And we said yes it probably did mean that those things might be a bit **TRICKIER**.

And then she said that in that case she would help us however she could. **WHOA!** We did not see THAT coming. **Serena Piffle** telling people not to buy her own **dad**'s **Handy Hands**™ in our **ASSEMBLY**, how brilliant was that? Then **Ivy** pointed out that whoever was in the **ASSEMBLY** could invite their parents along to watch and I was practically positive **Serena** looked like she was having a think about that. But it's always hard to tell.

The bit with the
assembly . . .

We were all so **EXCITED** when we got to school the next day – we had been practising the **ASSEMBLY** at home and I even practised on the phone to **Susie** and **Tom** and they *really* liked it (and **Susie** never EVER fibs).

Serena arrived in the hall *before* register and looked a bit Wibbly.

I *actually* felt quite **bad** for her. Doing the right thing was hard enough, but when it involved almost *certainly* getting into *trouble* with your **dad**, well then it was **SUPER hard**. It was *odd* to see her Wibbly as she usually makes **other people** feel that way and I **really** hoped I would *remember* this if she ever tried to do that to me again. But *somehow* I didn't feel that she would. At least not as much!

THIS JUST SEEMED TO MAKE MR PIFFLE'S EYEBROWS EVEN CROSSER . . .

BUT SERENA JUST CARRIED ON . . .

SO, YOU KNOW, LIKE, BUY LESS STUFF. LIKE, RILLY. LIKE, BUY LESS HANDY HANDS, BECAUSE, LIKE, WHAT IS ACTUALLY THE POINT OF THEM? I AM SURE I SPEAK FOR ALL OF US WHEN I SAY WE WOULD MUCH PREFER MY HAIR TO BE GREAT.

THEN THE CROWD WENT WILDER THAN WILD . . .

AND WE COULDN'T SEE MR PIFFLE'S EYEBROWS ANY MORE AS HE STORMED OUT OF THE HALL . . .

THE END.

ANG ON, DON'T FORGET ABOUT THE NOTICES . . .

TO BE CLEAR, OLLER BOOTS ARE NOT ACCEPTABLE SCHOOL UNIFORM.

NO ONE SEEMS TO HAVE SIGNED UP FOR HE SEMOLINA-EATING CHALLENGE ET. SO GET YOUR NAMES DOWN BEFORE YOU MISS OUT ON THIS, ERM, DELICIOUS OPPORTUNITY.

CAN WHOEVER IS STICKING GOOGLY EYES ON THE TOILETS PLEASE STOP? IT'S VERY OFF-PUTTING.

I'M SURE YOU ARE ALL INSPIRED BY THIS MARVELLOUS ASSEMBLY TO TAKE ACTION, SO GRAMPS IS RUNNING A PLACARD-MAKING WORKSHOP THIS AFTERNOON.

NOW IT'S THE END.

LATER ON . . .

Well, we had done our **BEST** and were all HOPPING with EXCITEMENT waiting for the evening paper to be delivered . . .

LOCAL NEWS

HANDS OFF THEIR FUTURE!

HANDS OFF OUR FUTURE

LOCAL CHILDREN PROTECT ENVIRONMENT

Planet-saving school assembly demands ACTION!

PLACARD-MAKING THIS WAY →

We were still so super EXCITED about being in the local paper the night before, and then *even* more super EXCITED that a BIG paper had *printed* the story that morning. Though it didn't stop us all being **SUPER** nervous that no one would come along to our **PROTEST**, even though **Gramps** had a full house for his placard-making workshop (EVEN the **EVIL** *dinner lady* came along). We had to stop **TEAM TOXIC** AKA **ToxiCo**, or at least get everyone to see what they were *really* doing. It was all SO **nerve-wracking**.

But we needn't have worried . . .

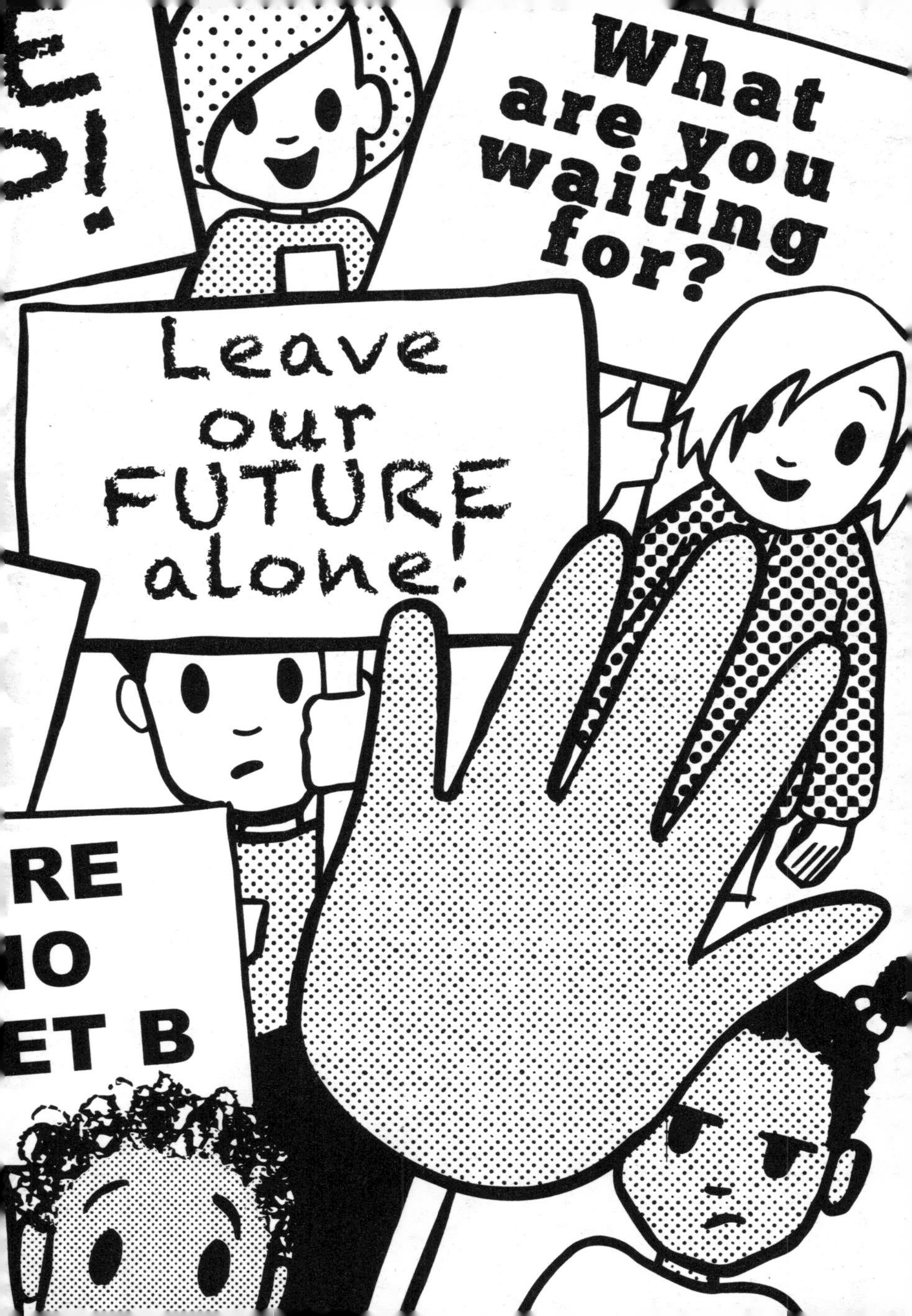
What are you waiting for?
Leave our FUTURE alone!

We couldn't **believe** that so many people had come along to the **HANDS OFF OUR FUTURE** protest. There were **lots** of people from school but **also** their grown-ups and some of their friends. It really felt like our craze was spreading. Ivy was right, we are good at crazes – it's just about picking the right one! *Even* the reporter from **ASSEMBLY** had come along and not just to report! She told us that thanks to the papers, news about our craze had started to *spread* already and there were lots of other protests and **S.A.N.D.W.I.C.H.E.S.** were popping up all over the place. **BRILLIANT!**

And I almost **exploded** with **happiness** when KAPOW and Perfecto turned up. I knew how much *trouble* they would get in for coming along but they had *anyway*, and I couldn't have been prouder to have them

as my *no-longer-secret* **BADDIE FRIENDS**. This business is so funny – everyone makes out there are just **goodies** and **BADDIES** but that just **isn't true** – and just as I was thinking that, **Serena** and **The Populars** walked up and joined us.

We might have been there for different reasons, **saving the planet**/being able to have great hair . . . but it **didn't matter** *exactly* why – we were all there *together*, because some things are just TOO important and our **future** (**future** future **OR** hairstyle future) was one of those things. We all just wanted the chance to be whoever we are going to be, **good** or **BADDISH**. And we were all united together to tell **Mr Piffle** and **TEAM TOXIC** AKA **ToxiCo** to take their *Handy Hands*™ **OFF OUR FUTURE**!

Just then some BIG blacked-out cars *arrived*, and it felt like the park protest all over again. I started to feel a bit **nervous** that I was going to have to use my jazz hands/glitter storm to protect everyone from **Mr Piffle** and his **BIG BUSINESS**, but it turned out I didn't have to. Just as he was getting out of his car, looking **FURIOUS**, **Serena** stepped *forward* and this stopped **Mr Piffle** in his tracks. I wondered if maybe **Serena** had **SUPER POWERS** after all and then she held up her hands and started *talking* . . .

Well, she **sort of** got it.

Yeah, OK, like, I didn't really pay much attention to the whole, like, climate change, planet-pollution thing before. I guess, it was, like, a bit sad-making and I don't really like feeling sad as you can probably tell from my constantly super happy expression. Yeah? And I was, like, totally busy with getting my hair done and shopping and being all round fabulous and fun stuff like that. But then, like, thanks to Pizazz and Ivy and all the other ones, I realised that if I don't pay attention and maybe actually get a little bit sad and even a bit cross then all the bad stuff that TEAM TOXIC / ToxiCo / my DAD are doing to the planet might mean no fun stuff at all. LIKE NONE! I have learned that we need to make better choices, maybe buy less stuff, but still be, like, really fabulous, yeah? And anyway, it's, like, REALLY embarrassing that your company is like totally mucking up the planet, Dad. And, like, totally uncool. And you don't want me to be UNCOOL do you, DAD? DAD? DAAAADDEEEEE??

I know that **SUPERHEROES** come in all shapes and sizes, but *Serena* really surprised us all. Maybe even herself. **Mr Piffle** looked surprised too or maybe that was just his **EXTRA FURIOUS** face, but whatever it was, he was listening. We all were. She was just coming to the end of her speech

when the sky went **DARK** and there was a **huge FLASH** . . . the **TEAM TOXIC** AKA **ToxiCo** space station had popped by. Great.

SMASHER, CAPTAIN NOTVERYNICE and **POLLUTOOOO** **ZOOMed** down and they were in a right **PROPER** STINK.

They marched straight over to *Serena* and her dad (whose face was now a bit *Wibbly*) and started giving him a right proper telling-off for letting us all get out of control! And couldn't he even manage a simple, highly **POLLUTiNG** craze like *Handy Hands*™? And come ON it was just silly kids anyway . . .

Well, that did it. SILLY KIDS? We were **not** SILLY KIDS. How **DARE** they dismiss us like that? It was us who had made secret **S.A.N.D.W.I.C.H.E.S.** . . . it was US who had made everyone see what was going on . . . it was US who had actually ROCKED **ASSEMBLY** the day before . . . it was US who had made it into the papers and got everyone **protesting** . . . it was US who had started a new **CRAZE**, one that would help PROTECT the planet's future, not help destroy it. SILLY KIDS?

Oh, I don't think so . . .

All of a sudden, I didn't feel nervous or even *slightly embarrassed*, I felt **proud** that I could use my jazz hands/glitter storm to SAVE my friends, to PROTECT the people and the planet that I **loved**. So I stepped forward, but just as I did, so did everyone else. We were all ready to use our **SUPER POWERS**, whether they were FIRE-BREATHING, *talking*, organising PROTESTS, **MAKING PLACARDS**, **showing up**, making *good* choices or even **jazz hands/glitter storms**.

TEAM TOXIC AKA **ToxiCo** looked **furious** and told **Mr Piffle** to hurry up and get on the **space station** so they could think of a new plan. But **Mr Piffle** actually hesitated. First of all I think the booing made him think twice, but **Serena** reached out her hands to him and showed him what she had written on them, what we had all written on our hands.

Plastico Fantastico HUFFED and demanded **Mr Piffle** make his mind up: go with them and make the big bucks/destroy the planet **OR** side with a bunch of SILLY KIDS. And while he took a little bit longer than any of us would have liked, **Mr Piffle** eventually looked down at **Serena**, who fluffed her hair, and he chose SILLY KIDS and quit **TEAM TOXIC** AKA **ToxiCo** for good.

WOW! **Mr Piffle** had made a *good* choice. Possibly his first! He was listening, finally, but better late than

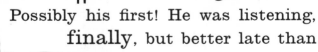

never. And if we could get him to *listen* then we could get almost **anyone** to *listen*.

Well, when he heard that, Plastico Fantastico went a funny colour and vowed TEAM TOXIC AKA ToxiCo would be back with an even better craze than *Handy Hands*™ and that would show us.

Then Ivy stepped forward and told TEAM TOXIC AKA ToxiCo that they will never win, because there is more *good* on this planet than *BAD*. And that us SILLY KIDS were just starting . . . to be a bit louder, and a bit braver. Then she said that actually our craze was now the NEW *sensation* sweeping the nation and it was about *caring* and *kindness* and telling real-life *BADDIES* . . . **HANDS OFF OUR FUTURE**.

Well, THAT did it.

They **scarpered**.

For NOW.

10

The bit where we all work some stuff out . . .

Well, of course we all *celebrated* with **pizza** and watched ourselves on the **ACTUAL TV NEWS**.

Our craze was *spreading* and we could not be happier about it. We decided to keep **S.A.N.D.W.I.C.H.E.S.** going, I mean this **battle** wasn't over. This was really just the **beginning**, but the most *important* thing was that we had made a **START**. None of us were perfect (not even **Perfecto**), and we wouldn't always make the *right* choice, but we would always try our best and **HELP** others to do the same. We couldn't **save the planet** on our own, but now we had each other and there were more **S.A.N.D.W.I.C.H.E.S.** joining us all the time, all over the place.

But just like **S.A.N.D.W.I.C.H.E.S.**, **TEAM TOXIC** AKA **ToxiCo** were going to keep *trying*.

NAME: CAPTAIN NOTVERYNICE
POWERS: BEING NOTVERYNICE
FAVE SNACK: PARMA VIOLETS
NEW JOB: BEING NOTVERYNICE
HOBBIES: GELLING HIS HAIR
BADDIE RATING: 356971

NAME: PLASTICO FANTASTICO
POWERS: MAKING STUFF PLASTIC
FAVE SNACK: BEEF CRISPS
NEW JOB: C.E.O.
HOBBIES: LAMINATING
BADDIE RATING: 356970

NAME: CAT-ASTROPHI
POWERS: CAUSING CHAOS
FAVE SNACK: CELERY
NEW JOB: FASHION EDITOR
HOBBIES: YELLING AT PEOPLE
BADDIE RATING: 789352

Though **some** of them did see the ERROR
of their ways and *tried* to make a **change** . . .

NAME: TERRY TOXIC
NEW POWERS: EXPERT USE OF A
HAIRDRYER
NEW JOB: HAIRDRESSER
HOBBIES: ASKING PEOPLE IF
THEY ARE GOING ON HOLIDAY
BADDIE RATING: 5

NAME: SEPTIC SQUIRREL
NEW POWERS: MAKING PEOPLE
LAUGH
FAVE SNACK: CHILLI NUTS
NEW JOB: STAND-UP
HOBBIES: KNITTING
BADDIE RATING: 3

NAME: SMASHER
NEW POWERS: HUGGING
FAVE SNACK: CAKE
(ANY CAKE.)
NEW JOB: HUGGER
HOBBIES: HUGGING
BADDIE RATING: 0

Serena and **The Populars** even officially joined the **S.A.N.D.W.I.C.H.E.S.** and **Mr Piffle** did his best to gather up all the *Handy Hands*™ and recycle them into actually **useful** things. He even started a new *initiative* with other **BIG BUSINESSES** to try to 'OUT-GREEN' each other. Like a competition. Only one where *everyone* wins. But **obviously** there was a big shiny trophy for the business that was GREENEST. *EYE ROLL*

SUNGLASSES

HOUSE BRICKS

CARPET

BOWLS

TRAINERS

DOG TOYS

FURNITURE

REUSABLE WATER BOTTLES

PLAYGROUND EQUIPMENT

PACKAGING

JEWELLERY

LESS PLASTIC GOES INTO THE OCEAN!!

MORE HANDY HANDS? NO!!

BUT PLASTIC CAN ONLY BE RECYCLED A FEW TIMES, SO ITS BEST TO AVOID IT IF YOU POSSIBLY CAN. OR ASK COMPANIES TO AVOID IT IN THE FIRST PLACE! POLITELY, OBVS!

THE BERNARDS invited **The Cheese S.A.N.D.W.I.C.H.E.S.** to *perform* as their warm-up act for the rest of the **tour**, STINK-EYE tipped them off (not so **STINKY** after all, eh?!) And while we couldn't make *all* of the shows, what with school, homework and **planet saving**, we **ZOOMED** in whenever we could. The rest of the **World Tour** was a huge success, but it was *great* to have them home *eventually*. STINK-EYE even cried. She said her right **EYE** was just being **extra STINKY** – but we knew!

KAPOW and **Perfecto** are still two of the bravest '*SUPERS*' I know, and I am almost sure **Mum** doesn't mind me having **BADDIE** friends. Because they helped us, **Aunty Fury** is keeping an eye on them. I mean it's tricky being a ***NOT-SO-BAD-BADDIE*** and if anyone *understands* that, it's **Aunty Fury**! **KAPOW**'s mum and **dad** are fine about it and are actually quite supportive. But **Perfecto**'s sister has put a lock on her door now. She won't tell **Perfecto** anything these days, but her **dad**, who had no idea about her ***NOT-SO-BAD-BADDINESS***, is *thrilled* as he is a ***NOT-SO-BAD-BADDIE*** himself.

And once everything had calmed down a little bit, we decided to have a *picnic* in the park next to school to *celebrate*, back where my **planet-saving** began (well, in an **ECO-COUNCIL** type way). It was so *lovely* to see everyone all together in a park that was very nearly a car park, feeling *good* about standing up to **TEAM TOXIC** AKA **ToxiCo** together and

winning!

Well, this time anyway.
I knew our **craze** was going
to spread *further* and *further* and
I felt so happy and proud of us
all, I couldn't help myself . . .

   I . . .
        I . . .

NICE

MONOLOGUED...

"I guess we all know that **TEAM TOXIC** AKA **ToxiCo** will be back and there will be more **Mr Piffles**, though they *probably* won't *actually* be called **Mr Piffle**... but now we are ready. Now we know what we have to do... work **TOGETHER** and **stand up** to those stinkers.

Protecting **our planet** and our future is a forever **battle** that we will fight every single day with the *choices* we make, the things we buy, the way we *support* each other and the way we live. But these are **SUPER** powers we all have and we all need to use them.

And while sometimes it can seem like there is just SO MUCH TO DO and it can feel like **A LOT**, we must *remember* the future is ours and we must protect it one little **battle** at a time.

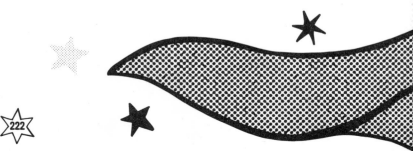

We must all **stand TOGETHER** and tell the **TEAM TOXIC**s of this universe:

HANDS OFF OUR FUTURE!!!"

And then I looked off into the middle distance and a *handy breeze* made my **CAPE** actually FLAP.

I was being

A

SUPERHERO

FOR

REAL!

The bit where YOU use YOUR super powers...

WE CAN **ALL** SAVE THE PLANET.
We can **all** be
SUPERHEROES.

The future really is in your hands!!!

While *sometimes* it can feel *overwhelming*, you must always remember you are NOT *powerless* – there are things you can do to help **save the planet** and you don't have to be a *SUPERHERO* with actual *SUPER POWERS* to do them. You have **more POWERS** than you know and it's time to use them.

It's YOUR **future**,

don't let

ANYONE

tell you otherwise.

WELL, MY LOVELY LOT OF SUPERHEROES, IT'S OVER TO YOU NOW. IT'S TIME TO USE YOUR SUPER POWERS TO SAVE THE PLANET . . .

MAKE SURE YOU USE REUSABLE SHOPPING BAGS, NO PLASTIC!

CUT DOWN ON PACKAGING. USE REFILLABLE WATER BOTTLES. JAM JARS MAKE GREAT STORAGE.

NO PLASTIC STRAWS! IF YOU MUST USE THEM, TRY METAL OR BAMBOO ONES . . .

OH, AND IF YOUR SUPER POWER IS JAZZ HANDS/GLITTER STORM THEN MAKE SURE YOUR GLITTER IS BIODEGRADABLE! NATCH!

CUT OUT CHEWING GUM, IT CONTAINS PLASTIC . . .

NO, THANKS.

GUM

EAT MORE VEG AND LESS MEAT . . .

RECYCLE YOUR FOOD WASTE

GROW YOUR OWN FOR FEWER FOOD MILES . .

NEVER DROP LITTER!

JOIN A LOCAL LITTER-PICKING GROU
MAKE SURE YOU DO IT SAFELY.

FEED THE BIRDS . . .

LEAVE A WILD PATCH IN YOUR GARDEN FOR BUGS AND BIRDS . . .

PUT WATER OUT FOR WILDLIF
BUT ADD SOME STICKS SO
ANY TRAPPED CREATURES
CAN CLIMB OUT . . .

BUY LESS FAST FASHION, TRY SECONDHAND INSTEAD!

MEND AND REFASHION OLD CLOTHES . . .

RECYCLE ANY GARMENTS THAT ARE BEYOND REPAIR . . .

RECYCLE EVERYTHING YOU CAN!

FIND THINGS YOU NEED, AND GIVE AWAY THINGS YOU DON'T IN YOUR LOCAL FREE PAPER.

BUY FROM SUSTAINABLE COMPANIES IF YOU CAN!

THESE ARE JUST SUGGESTIONS, AND IT'S NOT ALWAYS POSSIBLE TO DO THEM FOR ONE REASON OR ANOTHER. NONE OF US WILL GET IT RIGHT ALL THE TIME. BUT IF YOU TRY YOUR BEST AND MAKE CHANGES WHERE YOU CAN THAT IS AS MUCH AS ANYONE CAN DO. HOORAY FOR YOU! AND DON'T FORGET TO USE YOUR VOICE! IT'S YOUR PLANET TOO!

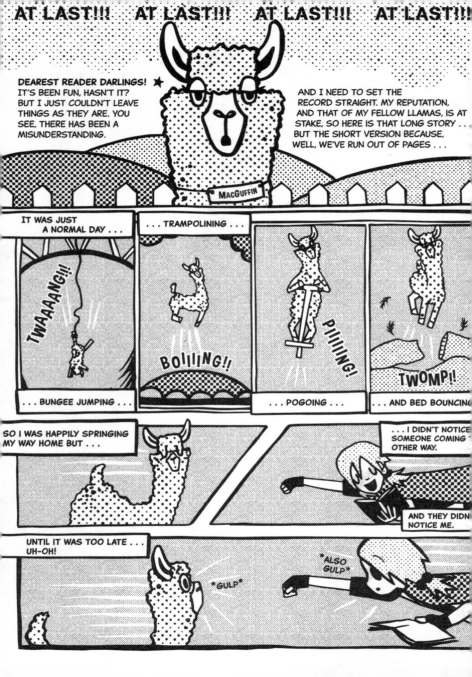

The End

Or is it?

Yes. Yes, it is.

Or IS it?

YES!

But is it, though?

Read all of PiZAZZ's SUPER ADVENTURES!

 Sophy Henn
is an **AWARD-WINNING**
author and illustrator with
a Masters in Illustration
from the University of Brighton. She is the
creator of the much-loved **BAD NANA** series,
the **POM POM** series, the **PIZAZZ** series, the **TED**
board book series, and the non-fiction **LIFESIZE**
series, among others. Her debut picture book
Where Bear? was nominated for the Kate
Greenaway Medal and shortlisted for the
Waterstones Children's Book Prize.

Sophy was the **WORLD BOOK DAY** illustrator in
2015 and 2016 and was a **WORLD BOOK DAY** author
in 2023. She writes and draws in her studio in
Sussex with a large cup of tea by her side and
can't quite believe her luck!